Vampires

by Janet Perry and Victor Gentle

This book is dedicated to the two Loren Stevens: to the one with whom (in her fantasies) the vampire Lestat may be secretly obsessed, and also to the gently ironic, graceful young woman known to the authors

Gareth Stevens Publishing
MILWAUKEE

For a free color catalog describing Gareth Stevens' list of high-quality books and multimedia programs, call 1-800-542-2595 (USA) or 1-800-461-9120 (Canada). Gareth Stevens Publishing's Fax: (414) 225-0377.

Library of Congress Cataloging-in-Publication Data

Perry, Janet, 1960-
    Vampires / by Janet Perry and Victor Gentle.
       p. cm. — (Monsters: an imagination library series)
    Includes bibliographical references (p. 22) and index.
    Summary: Discusses vampires in legend and literature and some real people and animals that may have helped inspire the concept of blood-drinking monsters.
    ISBN 0-8368-2442-3 (lib. bdg.)
    1. Vampires—Juvenile literature. [1. Vampires.] I. Gentle, Victor. II. Title. III. Series: Perry, Janet, 1960- Monsters.
GR830.V3P48   1999
398'.45—dc21
                            99-22509

First published in 1999 by
Gareth Stevens Publishing
1555 North RiverCenter Drive, Suite 201
Milwaukee, WI 53212 USA

Text: Janet Perry and Victor Gentle
Page layout: Janet Perry, Victor Gentle, and Helene Feider
Cover design: Joel Bucaro and Helene Feider
Series editor: Patricia Lantier-Sampon
Editorial assistant: Diane Laska

Photo credits: Cover, pp. 5, 7, 9, 15, 17 © Photofest; p. 11 © Archive Photos; p. 13 © Photofest/Jagarts; p. 19 © Archive/Fotos International; p. 21 © Mark Strickland/Innerspace Visions

Printed in the United States of America

1 2 3 4 5 6 7 8 9 03 02 01 00 99

TABLE OF CONTENTS

Words that appear in the glossary are printed in **boldface** type the first time they occur in the text.

"THE BLOOD IS THE LIFE" – Count Dracula

Hot breath near your throat! The stink of death! Your blood freezes. Two red, flaming eyes seize you in a trance. You feel weak and dreamy.

Alive the next morning? Barely! Your body is as hard to move as a bag of boulders. You had a bad dream, but you can't quite remember the details. There are two itchy holes in your neck!

"**Vampires**!" you gasp. "Blood-sucking monsters! Was I a vampire snack last night? Will I turn into a vampire?"

The vampire in the movie *Nosferatu* (1990) stops by for a midnight snack. Will his victim be drained of blood and die, or will she survive and become a vampire herself?

THE NUMBER ONE COUNT

The Scottish writer Bram Stoker created the most famous vampire of them all — Count Dracula. Stoker had learned about some terrible and cruel people who lived in Europe hundreds of years ago. He also studied beliefs about vampires. He used details from those beliefs to make Count Dracula really scary.

Here are some vampire features:

1. They can live forever.
2. They feed on blood, which gives them stinky breath.
3. They are super-strong and fast.
4. They were once human.

Some movies make fun of scary subjects. Here, Leslie Nielsen plays the lucky Count in *Dracula: Dead and Loving It!* (1995).

A REAL MONSTER, BUT NOT REALLY A VAMPIRE

Stoker named his vampire character *Dracula* after a man named Vlad Dracula, who lived long ago in eastern Europe.

Vlad's father, Vlad Dracul, was a fierce warrior. Vlad Dracula was worse: he was cruel. He stuck people on wooden stakes to **torture** and kill them. This is called **impaling**. He impaled his foes in battle. He impaled his own soldiers, too, if he thought they were cowards. He often impaled ordinary people for no reason at all. Vlad Dracula was also called Vlad Tepes, or "Vlad the Impaler."

Dracul means "dragon" or "devil." So, *Vlad Dracula* means "Vlad, son of the Devil." Vlad Dracula spilled lots of blood, even if he did not drink any.

8

Film director Francis Ford Coppola changed Stoker's story into a romance of love at first bite. Dracula falls in love with Mina. He believes she is his dead wife come back to life.

BLOODBATH BETH

Other actual people from history behaved in ways that remind us of the vampires we read about in stories.

One was the Hungarian countess Erzebet Báthory. About four hundred years ago, she kidnapped dozens of young women.

She tortured these women and let them slowly bleed to death. Many people think she drank and bathed in their blood. It's said she believed she would look young forever this way.

The Countess was tried and **convicted**. Her punishment was to stay in her own room for the rest of her life with the doors and windows sealed.

Countess Marya sees a **therapist** after claiming her father's body in *Dracula's Daughter*, a 1936 movie. Countess Báthory needed therapy, too.

HE WORKED FOR A SAINT, BUT WASN'T ONE

Baron Gilles de Rais was a general under Saint Joan of Arc, the French patriot. He was a great general, but a vicious man who kidnapped boys, cut their necks, and let them bleed to death. People say he drank their blood, but no one knows for sure.

He was caught, convicted, and beheaded for these terrible crimes.

Modern vampire stories use these histories. Using methods that remind us of Vlad Dracula and Gilles de Rais, vampires in stories are destroyed with a stake through the heart, or by chopping off the head. Like Báthory in her room, vampires must rest in their coffins, sealed tight against the light of day.

If you're near a castle where bloodthirsty vampires live, don't stop in for a bite! That's the lesson in *Kiss of the Vampire* (1963).

KISS OF THE VAMPIRE

in Eastman
COLOR

starring

CLIFFORD EVANS
NOEL WILLMAN
EDWARD DE SOUZA
JENNIFER DANIEL
BARRY WARREN

Screenplay by JOHN ELDER
Directed by DON SHARP
Produced by ANTHONY HINDS

A Hammer Film Production

A
Universal
Release

VAMPIRES AROUND THE WORLD

Most well-known vampires in modern stories are from eastern Europe. However, some vampire-like stories come from other parts of the world and far back in time. Here are some words for ancient vampires from around the world:

1. Babylon: *ekimmu*
2. Greece: *vrykolas*
3. Ireland: *dearg-due*
4. Japan: *nabeshima*
5. Malaya: *langsuir*
6. Scotland: *baobban sith*

Ancient vampires were all evil, but in some modern stories, vampires use their powers to fight evil. The hero of *Blacula* (1972) fights **racists** in Los Angeles.

TO KILL THE UNDEAD

Many stories about vampires tell how to destroy them in special ways; otherwise, the stories would never end. Those pesky vampires would live forever.

So, how do you destroy a vampire? If you were a vampire hunter in one of these stories, you would probably try these ideas first!

1. Expose the vampire to sunlight.
2. Drive a stake through the vampire's heart.
3. Chop off the vampire's head.

Not possible? Then you'd need some tricks just to keep the vampire from breathing down *your* neck. You might try using **garlic**, wild roses, a **crucifix**, holy water, or holy bread — then pray it works!

"Quick!" the vampire hunter thinks. "Drive in the stake! Ignore the screams as you release her soul. You must be cruel to be kind!"

CAN THAT MANY PEOPLE BE WRONG?

Most people today don't believe in vampires. Why have so many people believed in them in the past?

People may have gotten the idea of vampires from the effects of mysterious diseases, such as rabies. Rabies makes its victims pale. Light hurts their eyes. They become very thirsty. Rabies makes them insane, and they can bite others, infecting them, too.

Rabies victims can sleep so deeply, they might seem to be dead. They might wake up in their coffins and bang on the lids, frightening their loved ones.

Vampires behave, in some ways, like victims of rabies. If we in the audience didn't know he was a vampire, this man would just look like a very sick person.

REAL VAMPIRES

If drinking blood is what makes a vampire, then many creatures are vampires in this sense. Some even have the word *vampire* in their name!

Gnats, mosquitoes, fleas, and ticks all eat by sucking the blood of mammals. South American vampire bats make cuts on their hosts and lick the blood out of the wounds. Blood is nutritious for many living things.

We *humans* use blood in our food, too! Dishes like blood sausage and black pudding are made with the blood of goats and cattle. Yet, many people hate the idea of bloodshed of any kind. Do vampire stories fascinate us because we scare ourselves when we kill other animals for food?

This parrot fish has a "vampire snail" attached to its lip. The snail is actually sucking the blood out of the fish while it sleeps!

MORE TO READ, VIEW, AND LISTEN TO

Books (Nonfiction) *Informania: Vampires.* Martin Jenkins (Candlewick Press)
Meet the Vampire. Georgess McHargue (Lippincott)
Monsters (series). Janet Perry and Victor Gentle (Gareth Stevens)
Vampires: Opposing Viewpoints. Daniel C. Scavone
     (Greenhaven Press)

Books (Activity) *The Bunnicula Fun Book.* James Howe (Morrow Junior Books)

Books (Fiction) *Great-Uncle Dracula and the Dirty Rat.* Jayne Harvey
     (Random House)
Ma and Pa Dracula. Ann M. Martin (Holiday House)**
My Babysitter Goes Bats. Ann Hodgman (Pocket Books)
My Friend, the Vampire. Angela Sommer-Bodenburg
     (Dial Books for Young Readers)*
The Vampire Moves In. Angela Sommer-Bodenburg
     (Dial Books for Young Readers)*

Videos (Fiction) *Dracula.* (MCA Videocassette)
The Fearless Vampire Killers. (MGM/UA Home Video)
Nosferatu, the Vampire. (Blackhawk Films)
The Vampire Caper. (Walt Disney Home Video)

Play *The House of Dracula.* Martin Downing (Samuel French)

Audio (Nonfiction) *Dracula and Other Vampires.* Dr. Walter Starkie
     (National Public Radio)
Vampires. (National Public Radio)

Audio (Fiction) *Dr. Demento Presents Spooky Tunes and Scary Melodies.* (Rhino)
Vlad the Drac (The Adventures of a Vegetarian Vampire).
     Ann Jungman (Chivers Audio Books)

*also available in Spanish and German ** also available in Spanish

WEB SITES

If you have your own computer and Internet access, great! If not, most libraries have Internet access. Go to your library and enter the word *museums* into the library's preferred search engine. See if you can find a museum web page that has exhibits on bloodthirsty plants and animals and spirits who invade human bodies! If any of these museums are close by, you can visit them in person!

The Internet changes every day, and web sites come and go. We believe the sites we recommend here are likely to last, and give the best and most appropriate links for our readers to pursue their interest in the folklore of vampires, real or imagined, and related subjects.

www.ajkids.com

This is the junior *Ask Jeeves* site – it's a great research tool.

Some questions to try out in *Ask Jeeves Kids*:
- *Do vampire bats suck human blood?*
- *Where do I find animals that suck blood?*
- *Where can I find some good vampire and monster stories from Romania, or Japan, or China, or Scotland?*

You can also just type in words and phrases with "?" at the end, for example,
- *Vampires?*
- *Blood-sucking insects?*
- *Vlad Dracula?*

www.mzoo.com

The Miniature Zoo has a special section of monsters and weird critters. Go to the site and click on the Quick Site Index to see pictures and links to many strange and unusual bloodthirsty animals and insects!

www.yahooligans.com

This is the junior Yahoo! home page. Click on one of the listed topics (such as Around the World, Science and Nature, or Art and Entertainment) for more links. From Around the World, try Anthropology and Archaeology and Mythology and Folklore to find more sites about vampires. From Science and Nature, you might try the Health and Safety link to Diseases and Conditions and the History of Medicine. There, you can learn about how diseases spread, what you can do to avoid them, and how blood works. You might also find fun and disgusting facts about parasites and symbiosis. You can also search for more information by typing a word in the Yahooligans search engine. Some words to try are: *Erzebet Báthory, Vlad Dracula, Gilles de Rais, Bram Stoker,* and *vampires.*

GLOSSARY

You can find these words on the pages listed. Reading a word in a sentence helps you understand it even better.

convicted (kun-VIK-tid) — found guilty of a crime 10, 12

crucifix (KROO-sih-fiks) — a cross used for religious purposes 16

garlic (GAHR-lick) — a strong-smelling vegetable, a kind of onion, used in cooking. In vampire legends, garlic can keep vampires away 16

gnat (NAT) — a small, flying insect that bites people, other mammals, and birds to feed on their blood 20

impale (im-PAIL) — to force onto a sharpened stick or pole, or to drive a sharpened stick or pole into 8

racists (RAY-sistz) — people who treat other people differently, or even badly, just because they are of another race 14

therapist (THAIR-uh-pist) — a person whose job is to help others with emotional and mental problems 10

torture (TOR-chure) — to purposely cause pain in others, to force them to do something they do not want to, or just because the torturer likes causing pain 8, 10

vampire (VAM-pyer) — a creature of legends and horror stories, said to feed on human blood 4, 6, 8, 10, 12, 14, 16, 18, 20

INDEX

Careers For

Outdoor Types

Interviews by Andrew Kaplan

Photographs by Edward Keating and Carrie Boretz

CHOICES

The Millbrook Press

Brookfield, Connecticut

Produced in association with Agincourt Press.

Photographs by Edward Keating, except: John Jenkins (Natalie
Stultz), Paul Rasch (Charles Andre), Ann Schmitt (Carrie Boretz),
Billy Joe Tatum (Charles Andre).

Cataloging-in-Publication Data

Kaplan, Andrew.
Careers for outdoor types/interviews by Andrew Kaplan,
photographs by Edward Keating and Carrie Boretz.

64 p.; ill.: (Choices)
Bibliography: p.
Includes index.

Summary: Interviews with fourteen people who work in careers
of interest to young people who like to work in an
outdoor environment.
1. Outdoor life.   2. Vocational guidance — animal specialists.
3. Environmental protection.   4. Plants — Development.
I. Keating, Edward, ill.   II. Boretz, Carrie, ill.
III. Title.   IV. Series.
1991   796.5
ISBN 1-56294-022-8

Contents

Introduction

In this book, 14 people who work in outdoor-related fields talk about their careers — what their work involves, how they got started, and what they like (and dislike) about it. They tell you things you should know before beginning an outdoor-related career and show you how being an outdoor type can lead to many different kinds of jobs.

Many outdoor-related jobs are found in parks and rural areas — jobs such as park ranger, farmer, and rancher. But just as many can be found much closer to cities. Landscape architects and zoo curators, for instance, often work in, or near, major metropolitan areas. In addition, many outdoor jobs forsake the land entirely. If you like ocean breezes, you might want to be a marine archaeologist, a water sports instructor, or a Coast Guard seaman.

The 14 careers described here are just the beginning, so don't limit your sights. At the end of this book, you'll find short descriptions of a dozen more careers you may want to explore, as well as suggestions on how to get more information. There are many business opportunities to be found out of doors. If you're an outdoor type, you'll find a wide range of career choices open to you.

Joan B. Storey, M.B.A., M.S.W.
Series Career Consultant

"Zoos can replenish endangered animals in the wild."

MIKE DEE
ZOO CURATOR
Los Angeles, California

WHAT I DO:
I'm responsible for all of the mammals at the Los Angeles Zoo. I oversee a staff of forty-five animal keepers who feed and care for the animals on a daily basis. I'm also in charge of the zoo commissary, which provides food for all the animals.

My days include a lot of meetings. Sometimes I meet with other zoo administrators and we talk about the zoo's master plan. I also meet regularly with the keepers so they can talk to me about problems they've encountered, such as being unable to get the right food from the commissary or a health problem with a particular animal. Sometimes I meet with people from outside the zoo, such as officials from the U.S. Department of Agriculture who regulate zoos and people

from the Greater Los Angeles Zoo Association who teach classes on how to be a zoo volunteer. The zoo curators go over the class outlines to make sure the proper subjects are being taught.

When I'm not in meetings, I go out and check on the animals. I don't have regular rounds, the way a senior animal keeper does. But I make spot checks to see how the animals are doing.

HOW I GOT STARTED:
When I went to college, I studied biology. I wasn't sure what I wanted to do, but I thought I might become a biology teacher. I had a friend, though, with whom I shared an interest in reptiles. When he became a curator of reptiles at the zoo, I dropped out of school and began working here, too. I didn't work with reptiles, however. I got interested in mammals and birds instead.

When he is not in meetings, Mike checks on the animals.

Soon after I started work at the zoo, I was drafted into the army. But I asked the zoo to hold a job for me while I was away, and they did. When I got out of the army in 1970, I went back to the zoo and became an animal keeper. Then in 1976, I was promoted to senior animal keeper, responsible for thirteen other animal keepers. I began to do administrative things like give zoo tours to visiting dignitaries and attend meetings of the American Association of Zoological Parks and Aquariums. Since the zoo didn't have the funds to send people at my level to these meetings, I used my own money. But it was worth it. I learned a lot and met curators and administrators from other zoos. Eventually, in 1987, I was promoted to curator.

At the AAZPA meetings, I got the idea to travel and see for myself how animals lived in the wild, so that I could better care for them in captivity. I've been to India, Nepal, South America, Africa, and Indonesia. While one of these trips was at my own expense, the rest were paid for because I was a tour leader. I guided people through game parks, gave lectures, and so on.

HOW I FEEL ABOUT IT: The zoos of today are not what they were twenty years ago. Instead of a dead-end collection of animals going nowhere, zoos today are a reservoir that can be used to replenish the populations of endangered animals in the wild. We breed rare animals and put them back in their native environments. The golden lion tamarin, for example, is a critically endangered monkey. There are fewer than four hundred of them left in South America. With the help of other zoos, though, we've figured out a way to breed and then release

Mike oversees a staff of forty-five zoo keepers.

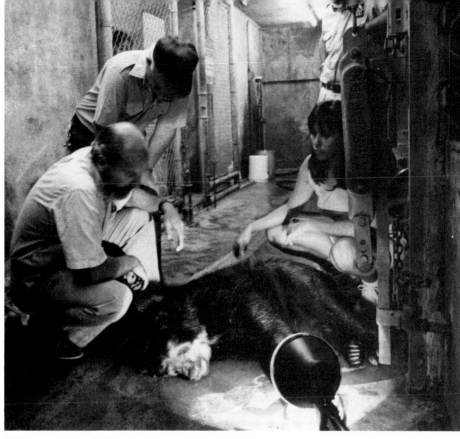
Mike and his staff care for a sick animal.

these monkeys into protected habitats in South America. So far, we've sent about fifty back. Our success is measured by the fact that they're breeding in the wild now and surviving.

WHAT YOU SHOULD KNOW:
Although many of our staff people have college educations, that doesn't count in our hiring decisions. What matters to us is experience with animals, and how people work with them. Our zoo has a sixteen-week animal keeper training program that's given twice a year.

Students in the program gain experience working with the animals, and their performance is evaluated by the keepers. The top students get jobs at the zoo. Some of our keepers, though, got their starts as volunteers.

The pay for zoo employees varies with the city. At our zoo, keepers start off at about $24,000. Curators at different zoos earn up to about $55,000, while directors can earn $70,000 or $80,000. Sometimes there are other perks, such as low-cost housing on zoo grounds. In addition, you can do consulting work.

"I like being part of the life process."

PEGGY MONZINGO
RANCHER

Benson, Arizona

WHAT I DO:

My son and I have a cattle ranch where I raise registered Hereford and commercial mixed-breed cattle. We're a cow-calf operation, which means that we raise our own calves to sell. Yearling operations, on the other hand, buy calves, raise them for a while, and then sell them.

On a ranch, your life revolves around your animals. Twice a day, we feed the cattle we have penned in the corrals. The rest of the time we take our horses and ride out to check on the rest of the cattle, looking to see whether any of them have gotten injured or been hurt by wild animals. Because our ranch consists of almost twenty thousand acres, my son and I have to do an awful lot of riding in order to keep track of what's happening.

Peggy tags all her cattle so she can identify them later.

Although twenty thousand acres might sound like a lot, it's not so large for this region. Because there's not much vegetation on the land around here, you have to have a big spread if you want to have enough forage for your animals. You might be able to keep ten head of cattle per acre in Missouri, but in Arizona you need an entire section, which is 640 acres.

Managing and improving the land is an important responsibility. Although my ranch is a mix of my own land, land leased from the state, and land leased from the federal government, I'm responsible for all the improvements. These include putting up fences, windmills, and water pipelines — and taking care of the land itself.

What I do is called renewable resource ranching. The cattle that aren't penned in graze freely on the ranch, eating grasses and plants

Peggy and her son do a great deal of riding.

that grow without our help — without irrigation, chemicals, or fertilizers. The only thing we do is move the cattle around so that the pastures can rejuvenate and the grasses can regrow. We're very serious about the condition of our land because we're in things for the long term. If we let the land get overgrazed, future generations of cattle will have no more food.

HOW I GOT STARTED:
I didn't start out on a ranch. I was raised on the East Coast, then got married and moved out to a ranch. Although I didn't know a thing about it, only how to ride a horse, I took to the life quickly. I really liked it, and I've been doing it since 1942.

I've been on three differ-ent ranches, and I've gotten further into ranching each time. The first ranch I worked on was in Arizona. After my first husband left, I ran that ranch myself for a time before I remarried and moved to New Mexico. Later, though, we moved back here to Arizona to be closer to family. Then my second husband died and I was running the ranch alone again. Now, things are a little easier because my son is old enough to run things.

HOW I FEEL ABOUT IT:
I like being part of the life process, the reproduction and renewal of animals and the land. I like having a cow-calf operation where we see the calves come every year. It's exciting to see the results

of our breeding decisions, and how our combinations of bulls and cows have worked out.

I often have to contend with problems like animal diseases, but they are really just part of the job. To me, the only real problem is politics. These days, you have to be involved in local, state, and federal politics. Because there are so few ranchers, you have a lot of people who don't understand ranching making decisions about it. You have to spend a lot of time countering their input.

WHAT YOU SHOULD KNOW:
Here in the West, you have to run a very self-sufficient operation because you're usually a long way from town. You need the skills, machinery, and parts to take care of your own vehicle maintenance, plumbing, and electrical work. You also need to know how to take care of everything on your property — fences, windmills, things like that — because you can't send out for a repairman so easily.

Also, this is not a nine-to-five, two-week-vacation sort of situation. Your hours are completely dependent on the cattle and the needs of your ranch. If a cow's having trouble having a calf, you go to help her. It doesn't matter if it's two in the morning. You're dealing with the life and death of an animal.

Ranching is a good life. It's hard to talk about the money because you plow almost all of it back into the ranch, making repairs or improving your herd. But you're on the land, and you have a good life.

Peggy feeds the cattle in the corrals twice a day.

"Artifacts are like Christmas presents. Each time, there's a surprise."

COREY MALCOM

MARINE ARCHAEOLOGIST

Key West, Florida

WHAT I DO:
I dive to the sites of sunken ships and look for artifacts, which I then preserve and study. Originally, I was with Treasure Salvors Incorporated, the group led by Mel Fisher that found and excavated the famous *Atocha* treasure galleon. Now I'm here at the Mel Fisher Maritime Heritage Society, which is a nonprofit arm of the same company. We work with the artifacts collected from the shipwreck, do research, and run a museum.

This kind of work follows a certain pattern. First you have to find the shipwreck. Because we've been working on Spanish galleons, someone had to go to Spain and look through four-hundred-year old documents for clues to the places where the Spanish lost ships. Next,

Corey retrieves an encrusted artifact from the sea.

boats are sent out to survey likely areas. Usually these boats tow magnetometers, which are large metal detectors that locate iron in the artifacts left by sunken ships. Once you've found a ship, you follow its trail, map the site, and dive to the wreck, bringing up what you find. Wrecks can be scattered over large distances. The *Atocha* wreck was scattered over more than ten miles in an area west of the Florida Keys.

As you might expect, this process can take quite a bit of time and cost quite a lot of money. One reason is the amount of territory that has to be covered during any search. Another is the work's archaeological aspect — you want to preserve and interpret the site as accurately as you can. To do this, you have to be very careful in your excavation so that you disturb the site as little as possible.

Corey examines one of the
artifacts he has recovered.

HOW I GOT STARTED:

When I was a child, I was
always interested in old
things like Indian arrow-
heads. And as for the sea, I've
always liked it. I learned to
dive long before I got involved
in this project.

I started working in the
field when I was 20 and
studying anthropology and
archaeology at a university.
My first job was as a technician on an archaeological
dig, digging in fields and

washing artifacts. It was part
of my degree work. Later I
worked at other sites, including a Georgia plantation and
some Indian ruins. Eventually I ended up at Key West
working on the *Atocha*
wreck. At that time, in 1985,
most of us were working in
the water. Now, although
some diving is still going on,
most of us are working in
the lab, studying what has
been found.

HOW I FEEL ABOUT IT:

I love diving, of course. On
every dive you learn something else, not just about the
ship but about the sea. You
see a fish you've never seen
before, and that's wonderful.
Beyond the diving, however,
I'm excited by the small,
unexpected discoveries I
make. Artifacts are kind of
like Christmas presents. They
are all so heavily encrusted,
and changed by being under-
water for so long, that you're
never quite sure what you're
going to find underneath.
Each time you clean some-
thing, there's a surprise. Once
I found a hammer unlike any
I'd ever seen. When I cleaned
it, I found out it was in perfect shape.

The only thing I'd like to
change about this work is
the public's perception of it.
The *Atocha* was a treasure
galleon, and we did find a lot
of gold and silver on it. But

we — the divers and the archaeologists — are not getting rich from it, and money isn't our primary focus.

A ship is like a little town unto itself. When we find one, we get valuable information about how people lived at sea. On the *Atocha*, we found everything that three hundred crewmen needed to live. Also, while we were looking for the *Atocha*, we found a slave ship called the *Henrietta Marie*, and that gave us valuable insights into African-American history.

WHAT YOU SHOULD KNOW:
To succeed at this work, you need a strong feeling for both history and the social sciences. You also need patience, an eye for detail, and the ability to improvise. Finally, if you're interested in undersea work, you should be comfortable with the ocean, and know how to dive before you start. Although it isn't hard to learn, there's a saying that it's easier to make an archaeologist into a diver than to make a diver into an archaeologist.

The hours and pay vary. When you're on the water, you have to work from sunrise to sunset, seven days a week, because it's expensive to run a boat. But once you're in the lab, you work regular eight-hour days. Starting pay averages about $20,000 a year.

After a dive, Corey cleans what he has found.

"One of the rewarding things is showing beginners they can windsurf, too."

TERRY O'SHEA

WINDSURFING TEACHER

Long Beach, California

WHAT I DO:
I'm the owner and director of a windsurfing school. I do everything — a lot of teaching, taking care of business, meeting with city officials to get permits and licenses, dealing with insurance problems, and taking care of finances. When I'm in the office taking care of the business, I have other instructors working for me down on the beach.

On a typical day, I go to the office and see who's scheduled for lessons that day. I call to confirm appointments. Then I head down to the school's beach location to prepare all the boards and equipment so that they're ready by the time the morning appointments start.

For the morning lesson, we start off talking about safety and basic sailing terminology. Then we put students onto a land simulator and work on posture and stance. The land simulator moves the way a board does in the water, only it's still on the beach. Once we've prepared the students, we put them out on the water and sail for a couple of hours. When they're done, we give them a few pointers and encourage them to come back and rent boards.

After the morning lesson, we take a short lunch break. Then we gear up for the second shift, which is a lot like the first except that we may have a few intermediate or advanced people. As the day winds down, I check with the local surf shops to see whether they need my brochures or have new people who are interested in lessons. Occasionally, I spend the whole day in the surf shops, meeting with past students and advising them on purchases.

Terry teaches beginners how to windsurf on a land simulator.

Terry shows a newcomer the proper way to hold the sail.

HOW I GOT STARTED:

When I was in college, I had a part-time job as a salesman in a surf shop. But I wanted to get out of the shop a little more, so I became the head instructor for the shop's sailboard school.

After I'd been teaching for a few years, the shop offered to sell me the school. They did this because windsurfing, being a physical activity, has a real potential for injury. You might swallow water or bump your head. While we haven't had much trouble with that, the store was worried about its liability because of rising court settlements and insurance costs. By selling the school to me, they got rid of their liability worries, and I got to be my own boss.

HOW I FEEL ABOUT IT:

Of course, I really like windsurfing. That's what got me started. But I also like teaching. One of the more rewarding things is showing beginners that they can windsurf, too. They come in and they're intimidated because they've seen pictures of people doing fancy loops and moves. But after just a few hours, they're windsurfing themselves. A lot of people are thrilled because they never thought they'd be able to do it.

The thing that bothers me the most, though, is the way the sport's portrayed in the media. Sometimes, cable sports channels show the very high end of the sport. They show guys with helmets and expensive equipment going at amazing speeds and doing aerial loops and tricks, which is very radical and intense-looking. But it's the opposite of what I'm trying to promote, which is the fact that everyone – the whole family – can do it. You don't have to be like crazed hang gliders. There's a calmer approach to the sport that's accessible to everyone, whether they're young or old, athletic or unathletic. For example, we teach people who have physical and learning disabilities to windsurf.

WHAT YOU SHOULD KNOW: You can get involved with windsurfing at an early age by hanging around a surf shop or a windsurfing school and doing errands. I have kids around here who help me with things like rigging the boards and greeting the customers. In return, I teach them about the sport and give them free board time.

The earnings potential is pretty open. In my geographic area, the business is seasonal — spring, summer, and fall — so I don't earn quite enough to cover the whole year. During the rest of the year, I work as a sales rep for a manufacturer of car racks that carry windsurfing equipment. However, someone who had schools in a few different counties, or had a year-round operation, could earn a pretty good yearly income.

Terry sails alongside some of the students.

"After my first rescue, I knew
I was in the right place."

KELLY TRACY

COAST GUARD SEAMAN

Portsmouth, New Hampshire

WHAT I DO:
Out of this station, we do mostly search-and-rescue and law enforcement work. Search and rescue involves towing disabled ships, putting out boat fires, rescuing people from capsized boats — that sort of thing. Sometimes there's an unusual situation, such as a diver being hit by a boat.

Another unusual situation is that President Bush has a house near here – in Kennebunkport, Maine – so we all do a fair amount of presidential security. For some people, that's the best part of the job. But to me it's just eight hours offshore in a boat, watching what goes on. The rest of the time we spend maintaining the boats and keeping the station in shape.

Everybody here is trained to do all the jobs because the station has to be open twenty-four hours a day in case of emergencies. Shifts are divided into two-day duty sections. You're here Monday and Tuesday around the clock, then you have Wednesday and Thursday off, and you're back here Friday through Sunday. The next week, it's the opposite.

HOW I GOT STARTED:
I grew up around the water, and I always liked the ocean and boats. As I got older, I decided I wanted to work on the water and to help people who got stranded. The Coast Guard was a natural choice. Besides that, the Coast Guard has a good program for sending people through college, and I wanted to take advantage of that.

I joined the Coast Guard after I graduated from high school. I had eight weeks of basic training and then on-the-job training at my

Kelly keeps a close watch for ships or people in trouble.

23

station. Everyone has to be qualified on a number of different boats, in tasks such as firefighting and seamanship, and in weapons. You also have to train with helicopters, learn the basics of first aid, and learn to work with the emergency medical technicians at the stations. Qualification takes from one to three months, depending on how motivated you are.

Besides boot camp and on-the-job training, there are also specialized Coast Guard schools, such as emergency medical technician school and law enforcement school. Whether you attend them is up to you.

HOW I FEEL ABOUT IT:

My favorite part of the job is helping people who are in trouble. I still remember the feeling I had on my first major rescue. A fishing boat had radioed in saying it was stuck on some rocks. There wasn't much visibility because it was nighttime, and the waves were ten feet high. The situation was pretty scary and if I had thought about it, I might have wondered whether I could go through with it. But you don't

Off duty, Kelly relaxes at the Coast Guard station.

Kelly charts a course in the pilothouse of a cutter.

have time for that. You get into the boat and do what you have to do. After that rescue, I knew I was in the right place, doing a job that was right for me.

Besides the work, I like the Coast Guard itself because it's fair. It's the only branch of the service in which men and women go to boot camp together. We get the same training, we're treated equally, and there's no favoritism among the personnel. Also, since we work so closely and on such long shifts, there's a bonding that goes on. We have the opportunity to build trust, and that's a major plus for me.

WHAT YOU SHOULD KNOW: Coast Guard service requires the ability to work with other people, and to trust them.

You have to be willing to put your life in another person's hands, and to gain the same kind of trust from them. If you can't do that, you can't be in the Coast Guard.

Base pay starts off at $900 per month, but the Coast Guard also takes care of your housing, gives you a food allowance, takes care of your medical costs, and offers college education benefits, which I'm taking advantage of.

The hours are the one thing that I would change if I could. Those overnight shifts are pretty difficult, especially when you're a single parent as I am. But the hours are really the only disadvantage I can think of, and that's pretty good when you consider the hours are necessary in the context of the job.

"I travel all over the world to places where people fish."

JOHN JENKINS
FISHING GUIDE
Burlington, Vermont

WHAT I DO:

I'm an outdoors writer, a photographer, and a specialty travel consultant, and I also guide sport fishermen on their trips. Although that may sound pretty far-flung, it all contains one common element: fishing. I'm a fisherman, and I travel all over the world to places where people fish. I write articles about where I've been and work with travel agencies that are interested in arranging fishing trips tours to these areas. Sometimes I return to these spots to guide other fishermen.

My projects develop in different ways. Sometimes a trip begins with a magazine's interest in a place, but ends in other types of work. For example, I was recently sent to Costa Rica by *Fishing World* magazine, which was

John fishes all over the world in both fresh and saltwater.

paying me to do an article on a fishing camp down there. While I was in Costa Rica, however, I also took photographs. And when I got back, I served as a consultant for a travel agency here that also wanted information on fishing in Costa Rica.

Other projects can develop out of my travel consultant work. For example, a travel agency or a developer may pay me to investigate the fishing and resort potential of a particular area or a particular group of islands. I'll go there, report back to my client, and then write articles for magazines on what I've seen. Later, if a lodge is developed, I may return to the area to act as a guide. This type of situation developed for me in the Los Roques Islands, where I served as a consultant and trained guides. Now, I've been given the opportunity to act as a head guide for a fishing camp there.

27

HOW I GOT STARTED:

I was raised fishing. I fished all over southern Connecticut – in the ponds, the rivers, any place I could hitchhike to – and in Long Island Sound, where my family had a boat. Also, my father would take us up to Cape Cod every

John uses a fly rod to cast for trout in a Vermont stream.

summer, and we'd fish a few more weeks there. Fishing's been a passion with me since I was 6, and only developed into a vocation later on.

I was also raised in an atmosphere of books and ideas that gave me a respect for writing. I went to the University of Vermont, where I majored in English and art history. When I graduated, I decided to look into publishing careers, and that led to the kind of work I do now.

My first job, at *Salt Water Sportsman*, put my interests together. As special projects editor, I edited articles, captioned photographs, and also wrote my own reviews and feature articles. My experience at this magazine gave me the background I needed to go off on my own and work freelance.

HOW I FEEL ABOUT IT:

I enjoy so many different aspects of my work. It gives me the opportunity to travel and to fish all over the world in many exotic locations. I go to places that are relatively untouched and uncrowded, where the fishing has been diminished less by commercial fishing, pollution, habitat destruction, or sheer numbers of fishermen. I also get to see and experience different cultures in a way that the average traveler usually doesn't.

John writes articles about the places he has been.

WHAT YOU SHOULD KNOW: There are several different ways to break into this kind of work. You can get a magazine job, as I did. Or you can go straight to writing freelance articles. To do that, you first have to decide what you know best. For example, if you're interested in fishing, you should get to know the nearby species and situations. Then you should think of a sentence that sums up a situation, and take your idea to the editor of a local magazine. As you write, you'll build up your credits and expand your contacts and your work.

Freelancers have no set routine or salary. For myself, the year divides this way: one third is spent keeping in touch with contacts and making arrangements; another third is spent afield, doing assessments and guiding; and the last third is spent writing articles and assembling photographs.

The money that you make depends on how much you work and your standing in the field. A good travel writer with some contacts who works steadily may make $30,000. At the other end of the spectrum, there are people who through their books, slide shows, guiding jobs, and consulting work make over $250,000 a year. There are probably about eighteen people who fall into that category, and they are all very well known.

"What we do on a
day-to-day basis
depends on the time
of year."

RICH TRACY
WINEMAKER
St. Helena, California

WHAT I DO:
I oversee all the wine production at Folie-à-Deux winery, manage the vineyard, and supervise the marketing staff. We often buy grapes from other vineyards, so I'm responsible for that, too.

What we do on a day-to-day basis depends on the time of year. In January, we prune in the vineyard. Then as spring arrives, we tie and train the vines and cultivate the soil. By July, if we're all caught up on the vineyard work, we take a break and wait six to eight weeks for the harvest.

In August, we start taking berry samples from our own vineyard and the vineyards we buy from. We do this to determine how the maturation of the grapes is progressing. From this we can tell when the proper time to pick

Rich monitors all the wine produced at his vineyard.

them will be. Once the grapes are harvested, I make sure that they're properly handled, crushed, and processed. Then we do the winemaking.

Bottling and marketing also follow cycles. In January, we bottle champagne. In June, we bottle a red wine and our chardonnay, which is a white wine. However, we don't sell these wines until almost a year later, so in the winter and spring after they're bottled, there's a big marketing push to sell them and I do some traveling.

HOW I GOT STARTED:
Originally, I was a pre-med student at Oregon State University. But in my senior year, I met my future wife, who convinced me to switch to science education. After we got married, we moved to California, where my wife's father was starting a vineyard.

In California, I began a

31

Rich often tours the vineyard to check on the grapes.

master's program in education and took a few elective courses in growing grapes and making wine so that I could talk about winemaking with my father-in-law. At that time, however, the California wine industry was beginning a period of major growth. Eventually, I switched majors and got a master's degree in horticulture, specializing in viticulture — the cultivation of grapes.

HOW I FEEL ABOUT IT:
I like the diversity in the job. Since this is a small winery, I get involved with everything. At a large winery, my job would be to supervise the people who do the actual winemaking. At this level, I do both — I supervise winemaking and I make wine. In addition, I'm involved with the marketing, and I develop labels, names, and brochures. As a result, there's a lot of creativity involved.

The problematic part of this work, however, is dealing with the county. It has regulations that are designed to protect the region from overdevelopment — and for the most part, that's a good idea. However, it can make things difficult. For example, if we want to expand our operation, we need to get a use permit and complete all the planning paperwork that's involved with that. Then once we get the permit, we have to begin all the construction within 180 days. You can't stagger it. This, plus the planning, translates into a lot of money. Things can get tight, which forces us to market our wines at times with discount structures.

WHAT YOU SHOULD KNOW:
As with most industries, the best way to start out is to get some on-the-job experience, either part time or by volunteering. Kids who live near a winery can come in and work. A ninth grader does our computer programming. I also know an eighth grader who does filing for a grape warehouse. Both of these kids are getting an idea of what the business is like and how it works.

In college, it's a good idea to study science and business. The science provides important background for graduate school studies in grape growing and winemaking. But the business is important, too, because it's a big part of the work, and it's better if you don't have to learn it on the job.

After college, there are several ways to get into this work. On the viticulture side, some people start out as part of a field crew at a vineyard. Others work for wineries, gathering berry samples and checking grapes during the harvest. And still others work in labs doing analysis.

Winemakers work long hours that get longer during harvesttime. I've worked some harvests when I've had just two hours of sleep in four days. Salaries depend on the size of the operation. Winemakers make from $20,000 to more than $60,000 at a large winery, and even more if they own their own wineries.

Rich oversees the bottling and storage of the wines.

"This is a place where you can really make friends, young and old."

LOUIS MAUNUPAU
RECREATION DIRECTOR
San Francisco, California

WHAT I DO:
I oversee all the sports activities at a neighborhood park in San Francisco. I put together baseball, basketball, football, and soccer teams for city-wide leagues, and I also set up tennis lessons and tournaments for the people who play at the courts here.

The leagues I work with are run by the athletics division of the parks department, which sends out notices to every park and recreation center in the city. If your park can field a team, you sign the kids up. The Parks and Recreation Department League works the way any organized league does, with rosters and schedules. I coach and manage all the teams from my park, run the practices, and go to all the games.

Louis teaches neighborhood children about recycling.

I also help with the maintenance of the park. Technically, this is not part of my job, but I am supposed to make sure that the park is safe. For example, when the gardener isn't around and I see glass in the children's play area, I clean it up. Or if I think that some of the apparatus is dangerous, I do something about it, either fix it myself or requisition repairs.

HOW I GOT STARTED:
Until I was about 12, I was small, sickly, and not very involved with sports. But then, in the next year, I grew about thirteen inches. Also, my health improved and I began going down to the park to play football, basketball, and tennis with my friends.

I continued athletics in college, where I became a varsity football and tennis player. I also started working part-time in the park, which was perfect for me. After col-

35

Louis makes sure his park is safe and enjoyable.

lege, I tried some other jobs. But I eventually came back to the park and, by picking up work as a substitute in other parks, turned it into a full-time job.

HOW I FEEL ABOUT IT: This job has a lot of benefits, some of which are more obvious than others. As you might expect, I like working outdoors, and being involved with sports. But there are other advantages to a park environment, advantages that you might not think of. This is a relaxed atmosphere — I don't have a boss or a dress code. And more importantly, it's a place where you can really make friends, both young and old. You see the same people every day, and your common denominator is sports and having fun. It's a better basis for true friendship than most jobs provide.

Another unique aspect of my job is its non-financial nature. Although people's tax dollars pay my salary, park users themselves don't pay me directly, so my relationships with people are free of that problem. People come to the park, and I'm there to help them in every way I can. If they're taking tennis lessons, I can be honest and open in a way that a club pro might not be. As far as the team sports, I'm not under the kind of pressure that a college coach is — my teams don't have to win. I'm just there to see that the kids have a good time, try their hardest, and get all the enjoyment and benefits they can out of the park and the sport.

One drawback to this type of work is that you can't really make it your life's work. As a young single person, I can afford to live on the $9.95 an hour that I make. But to make enough money to support a family, I would have to go into parks administration, which would mean working in an office instead of out in the park. It really wouldn't be the same type of work anymore. It would be bureaucratic work, which I don't like.

WHAT YOU SHOULD KNOW: The hours vary according to the season. In the job description, my position is thirty-six hours per week in the summer, and twenty-six hours per week the rest of the year. But to be a good parks director, you need to put in more time than that. For example, on a Saturday morning I might have to be at another park to coach one of our teams. So I come to my park early to open it and set things up. I put up a sign telling people where I am, and then go to my game.

Sometimes there may be a large picnic going on. Although I'm supposed to close up the park and its bathrooms at five, I don't do that. I leave it open for the people to use. Instead, I come back later, at eight maybe, to lock the park up. I'm not paid for this. But I do it because I love the park, and being part of the community.

Louis gives tennis lessons and plans the park tournaments.

"I'm happy because I'm out in the elements."

BETTY ANN LISTOWICH
SKI PATROL
Kingfield, Maine

WHAT I DO:
From early November through mid-April, I patrol the slopes at Sugarloaf, which is a ski resort in Maine. The ski patrol is responsible for the safety of the trails. When the first snowfall comes and the season gets underway, we check out the trails to get them ready to open. Once the season begins, we're due on the mountain anywhere from 7:00 to 8:30 in the morning. We check out the lifts and make sure they're running properly. Then we do morning trail checks to see that the trails were groomed properly the night before. After that, we ski the mountain all through the day to make sure that everything's safe. We put up fencing around lifts, mark unsafe intersections and hazards, and clear trails of any debris. At the end of the day, we sweep the mountain. We ski every trail, meet at each intersection, and make sure that nobody's left on the hill.

Besides all these tasks, there's a lot of public contact. People ask us for advice and comment on the trails and the lifts. We also do a lot of accident prevention. If people are skiing recklessly, we speak to them and, if necessary, take them off the mountain. Obviously, we help anyone who's injured. We're trained in a first-aid system called WEC – Winter Emergency Care – that's geared specifically to the outdoors. We pride ourselves on our ability to get injured people off the mountain quickly and safely.

HOW I GOT STARTED:
I started skiing when I was 7. My father, brother, sister, and I all learned at the same

Betty Ann makes sure that the lifts are running properly.

39

Betty Ann files smooth the edges of her skis.

time. One Christmas we all got skis and tried them on a nearby hill. I've been skiing ever since.

When I was in college, I started skiing here at Sugarloaf. After college, I got a job waitressing, mainly so that I could ski all day. But I got tired of working indoors and at night all the time. So I got a job with the ski patrol instead.

Sugarloaf isn't my only source of income, however. Although I work here as a patroller, and my husband works here as a trail groomer, we also run a plant nursery and landscaping business during the off-season. We started it about eight years ago, and it's just another way we're able to combine our love of the outdoors with practical skills that earn an income.

HOW I FEEL ABOUT IT:
I like getting out of bed in the morning. Whether it's the winter and I'm headed to the mountain, or the summer and I'm headed for the garden, I'm happy because I'm out in the elements. To me, there's nothing better. I love being on the mountain in a blinding snowstorm or windstorm, and I've developed a relationship with the environment so that I can tell from the wind and the color of the sky when a storm is coming or when things will be clearing up.

WHAT YOU SHOULD KNOW:
Being a good ski patroller takes a lot more than skiing ability and a knowledge of first aid. You have to have a good sense of judgment because there's a lot of calls that have to be made on your own. You also have to be calm under pressure. And finally, because this job puts you in touch with everyone — groomers, lift mechanics, medical personnel, and skiers — you have to be able to get along with many different types of people.

In addition to the personal characteristics I've mentioned, there's a lot of specific training involved. During your first year, you're monitored and trained by the other patrollers. After that, you participate in ongoing educational programs on the mountain, including a yearly fall refresher program in first-aid and lift-evacuation techniques. There are also demonstrations and lectures given throughout the year.

You won't get rich doing this. Ski patrollers start at about $6.00 an hour and make up to about $8.00 an hour. It's not a bad wage for this area of the country, but when you consider the technical knowledge you need, it's not too high. However, for most of us, money isn't the bottom line. We're here because we like it. I do other work so that I can afford to be here. We also work with volunteer patrollers, who have other jobs but work here because they like being on the mountain.

Betty Ann makes notes on the trail conditions.

"Working in a forest has rewards that you can't find anywhere else."

GARY CARR

RANGER

Gorham, New Hampshire

WHAT I DO:

I'm a district ranger in the White Mountain National Forest in New Hampshire. The forest is divided into five districts, and I have the overall responsibility for one of them. A staff of about thirty people — half permanent employees and half seasonal employees and volunteers — helps me do my job. Together, we take care of 126,000 acres of forest and serve the people who use it.

This job is a combination of outdoor work and administrative duties. When I'm lucky, I get outside about three days a week checking the trails, the campgrounds, the beach area, and the sites where timber is cut. At other times, I might spend all my days inside. For example, I might have staff meetings and be involved with fire-

training sessions for people learning to work on the fire-control crew.

I also spend a lot of time indoors working on the district budget and the annual sale of six million board feet of forest timber. It's a big job involving lots of negotiations and complicated contracts, but I have a staff who help me with it. They help me make sure that things are done properly — that erosion control is taken care of, that the wood is removed properly, and that no additional timber is damaged or stolen.

Aside from working with my staff, I also work with cooperators, which are nonprofit organizations that help out in the forest. The Appalachian Mountain Club is a good example of one of these groups. Its members do trail work and run a visitor center where forest users can get food, lodging, and useful information.

Gary's job involves a lot of administrative work.

HOW I GOT STARTED:

My grandparents had a farm and I spent a lot of time there fishing and hunting, which stimulated my interest in wildlife and the outdoors. When I went to college, I decided to learn about the environment, so I got a B.A. in wildlife biology. Then I studied an extra year for a B.A. in forestry, which is the study of the forest as a renewable resource. You learn about plants and trees, and the engineering involved with building roads and mapping forests.

After college, I went to work for the National Forest system at the Mark Twain National Forest in southern Missouri. My career was interrupted by three years in the army, but when I got back I spent a year at the Nicolet National Forest in northern Wisconsin and then became forest biologist here at White Mountain. I did land appraising and timber management in Michigan for a time, but I finally moved back here to be district ranger. Altogether, I've been in this work for twenty-eight years.

HOW I FEEL ABOUT IT:

I enjoy dealing with the public, but I also like watching the forest go through its cycles and its changes. It's rewarding to work in a forest because it feels as though you're helping to preserve it.

The two things that bother me the most are the arbitrariness of the budget process and the abuse of the forest. My budget passes through a lot of hands, and it's often well into the year before I know exactly how much money I have to work with. And as for forest abuse, some forest users don't care at all about fouling their own nest. Fortunately, most people aren't like that.

WHAT YOU SHOULD KNOW:
To become a forester or a ranger, you should get as extensive a background as possible. Besides a knowledge of forestry, communications and writing skills are necessary to deal with the public. Also, the field of environmental law is expanding, so you need to be knowledgeable and flexible enough to talk to lawyers, officials, and environmental activists.

Besides schooling, it's important to get as much hands-on experience as possible. That's where summer jobs come in. You should strive for variety. Forests are different from region to region, and you should try to work in as many different regions as possible.

Like most jobs, the hours and pay expand as you move up. The pay scale in the National Forest system is the same throughout the country, so the pay goes further depending on where you are. In a rural area, this is a good living; in a more expensive area, the pay isn't as rewarding. A starting forester makes $15,000 or $16,000. A district ranger can make about $40,000. If all you're looking for is money, this isn't the place. But working in a forest has other rewards that you can't find anywhere else.

Gary examines one of the sites where timber has been cut.

"The time I spend alone in the woods gives me a peace and solace that I can't find anywhere else."

BILLY JOE TATUM
NATURALIST
Melbourne, Arkansas

WHAT I DO:
I specialize in the study of edible and medicinal plants. A lot of my time is spent out in the countryside, foraging for and identifying these plants. Based on what I find, I give lectures and slide shows and supervise field trips. I also write articles and books about the history, folklore, and cooking of the Ozarks and elsewhere.

I give lectures to many different kinds of audiences. I speak at colleges and universities, and guide students from these places on trips. I also work with state park systems and various private organizations – such as Lion's Clubs, garden clubs, and herb societies. In addition, there's a facility near here called the Ozark Folk Center that's devoted to the

survival of such Ozark crafts as herb growing, cooking, basket making, and furniture making. The center is nationally known, and through my work there I'm exposed to a lot of people.

There's no such thing as a typical day or week for me. Sometimes I'm so busy lecturing and writing that I don't spend as much time outside as I'd like. On the other hand, in the mushroom season, I'm sometimes outside eight or ten hours a day. In the winter, I might be out of the state or even out of the country, researching different areas, foraging for food, and talking to different people about what they eat.

HOW I GOT STARTED:
I think it's important for people to enjoy and appreciate the place where they live, so when my kids and I moved to a tiny town with creeks and woods nearby, I took

them exploring so they could find and collect things. As they discovered the countryside, I discovered along with them. This was the real beginning of my work with plants.

Around the same time, my husband, who is a doctor, began collecting home remedies from his patients. These were sometimes herbal treatments, passed down from parent to child through many generations. Gradually we discovered that his patients knew a lot about the edible plants that my kids and I were investigating. Through them, and the work of naturalists such as Euell Gibbons, I learned about the plants myself.

Later, we moved further back into the country. My children were all in school then, and I had all day to myself, so I spent even more time in the woods. I also learned to write articles and began writing for *Ozarks Mountaineer* magazine and other publications. Through my writings, including three books, and my work at the Ozark Folk Center, I made contact with lots of people and soon found myself lecturing, leading field trips, and writing reviews and articles. Over the years, I've been written up in *People* magazine, *National Geographic*, and many other

Billy Joe forages for plants in the Arkansas countryside.

magazines and newspapers. I've also been on Johnny Carson and other television programs.

HOW I FEEL ABOUT IT:
In many respects, this work is very good for me. The time that I spend alone in the woods gives me a peace and a solace that I can't find anywhere else. My time is my own. When I'm writing, I'm able to write at any speed I want and get published when and where I want. That helps me avoid feelings of pressure and anxiety.

At this point, lectures and tours take more out of me than they put into me. Like any job, if you do something over and over again, it gets to be a habit. However, when I

48

do these things, I try to keep my enthusiasm high. I try to remind myself of the feeling I had when I first learned about these things, and then communicate this excitement to the people I'm with.

WHAT YOU SHOULD KNOW: This particular field – plant study and nature writing – is more about being interested and observant than it is about anything else. Naturally, if you have a degree in something such as natural history, biology, or medicine, it simplifies things. But if you have an interest, as I do, you'll learn what you need to know regardless of what your formal schooling is.

Many people who are interested in edible plants make their livings from writing articles, field guides, and books on the subject. However, there are also people who make their livings as collectors and seed gatherers. While you can buy packets of seeds for many kinds of plants, there are many rare varieties that aren't readily available. So some people collect seeds from rare and endangered plants, and sell them. One person I know collects seeds and sells them by mail. His earnings from that are a substantial part of his income.

Billy Joe is always trying to identify new plants.

"There's no split between job, home, and interests. I'm living my interests every day."

PAUL RASCH

ORGANIC FARMER

Fox, Arkansas

WHAT I DO:
I'm the farm coordinator at Meadowcreek, which is a nonprofit environmental center. We run the farm here using alternative, environmentally sound techniques, and live off what we produce. We also run agricultural and environmental education programs that draw students from all over the world. Although our educational programs vary in length, focus, and the students they attract, they're all a combination of classroom study and field experience, and they all cover some aspect of land use.

The unique thing about Meadowcreek is that we don't look for solutions to environmental problems only in the classroom. When we talk about an agricultural problem, for example, or a problem in forestry, students can

actually see the solutions that we've found on the farm.

Something else they see is how this farm supports the seven households on it. Our community here is very concerned with the field of alternative energy – energy conservation, renewable energy sources, and alternative waste management. We talk a lot about these subjects in the classroom. But we also show our students viable approaches that we utilize ourselves. For example, all of our facilities are solar- and wood-heated.

The people who work at Meadowcreek all have responsibilities in connection with the program. As farm coordinator, I'm responsible for managing the operation of our 1,500 acres. We have other people in charge of our cattle, forest, and market garden operations. In the classroom, the educational programs are a shared responsibility, and we each have lectures and subject areas for which we're responsible. But once the students are in the field, then I'm responsible.

HOW I GOT STARTED:

I grew up on a farm, and now I'm back on a farm, but in between I took a kind of a detour. I went to school at a place called the Land Institute, a small research center in Kansas that specializes in alternative agriculture. I studied solar engineering there. The Institute is a lot like Meadowcreek in that it addresses many of the same issues. But unlike Meadow-

creek, its focus is on research rather than on education.

HOW I FEEL ABOUT IT:

I like the way of life here. There's no split between job, home, and interests. I'm living my interests every day. I'm outdoors, which I love, and I'm still close to my family. I even take my two-year-old son out to the fields with me when I'm doing my work.

Another positive aspect of Meadowcreek is that it's both a farm and a teaching institution. As a result, there's a lot of diversity in terms of the work and the people. I have both the solitude of farming by myself

When he is not teaching, Paul tends the crops.

As farm coordinator, Paul is responsible for 1,500 acres.

and the chance to work with others.

Meadowcreek's biggest problem is also its biggest challenge – money. This country has the cheapest food prices in the world, so it's difficult for a place like Meadowcreek to compete with large farms that are cheaper to operate because they're less ecologically sensitive. It would be a lot easier if our society was willing to pay more for food so that we could encourage more responsible land use. But this isn't happening, and we can't be a viable demonstration if we can't show that our methods make both economic and ecological sense. Instead, we try to meet the challenge by balancing ecological necessity with economic reality.

WHAT YOU SHOULD KNOW: Farming is hard to compare to other kinds of work. Because you live where you work, it doesn't really make sense to talk about this job's hours. The economics of farming are also difficult to pin down. Here in the Ozarks, I know some people who work very little – maybe ten hours a week – and earn almost nothing. But they survive because they grow their own food and are self-sufficient. And I know other farmers who make a modern salary. What you earn depends on your knowledge of farming and markets and your willingness to work. If you're experienced, I think that it's not too hard to make $30,000 or $40,000 on a manageable piece of land.

People who are interested in farming should get out there and get as much experience as possible. Get in touch with the land. Take walks in the woods. Most importantly, pitch in on farms. Older farmers know a lot about the land, and how to grow things on it without using fossil fuels the way corporate farms do. These people can really teach you more than textbooks.

"You can work on big national parks, be a city planner, or do garden design."

ANN SCHMITT

LANDSCAPE ARCHITECT

Greenwich, Connecticut

WHAT I DO:

I'm a landscape architect, which means that I'm a type of artist. Many people think we dig holes and put in plants. That is the work of a landscape contractor. Landscape architects can be thought of as similar to traditional architects. We're interested in how to use a piece of land so that it works well and looks good.

Landscape architecture is a very broad field. Our firm, for instance, does small-scale work — that is, we do residences, public parks, and the grounds of office buildings, as well as town and regional planning. An architect designs the building, and we design all the elements of the built landscape.

With a residence, the owner might want to add a swimming pool, a deck, and

some trees. We evaluate and plan the site, produce the construction drawings and specifications, process any required government permits, and put the contract out for competitive bid to contractors. Then we observe the work done by the selected contractors to make sure that our drawings are being followed. We also approve the bills of the landscaper, electrician, and so on, to make sure the client has only been billed for what has been done. Finally, we draw up a maintenance schedule for the client to follow in taking care of the new space.

Our firm has two landscape architects, two trainees, and an office manager. We have a weekly meeting to talk over our work on projects for the next week. Then we parcel out the work. The work might involve going out to a site in the morning, then spending part of the day in the office

Ann surveys the site before designing the landscape.

at the drafting table. Now-adays computer drafting is becoming more common. It's great because it saves time. We don't have to redraw plans from scratch. We can make changes in a minute, and the printout always looks good.

HOW I GOT STARTED:
In high school I thought it would be great to design gardens, but I didn't think people got paid for it. Then I heard of landscape architecture. I met a woman who was a landscape architect. I saw some of her work, her office, her drawings, and I liked it.

I went to the Agriculture School at Cornell University and majored in landscape architecture. It's very much like an architecture program, but there's a wider variety of training. I studied three major areas in college: design, civil engineering, and botany. After you graduate, you have to get licensed by your state. To do this, you must serve as an apprentice for a couple of years, then you take a state exam.

HOW I FEEL ABOUT IT:
The work is challenging and varied. There are aspects that you don't think about when you're in school. For example, you often have to be a mediator among the client, the government, and the contractors. You have to be

Anne works on the plans for a site at her drafting table.

diplomatic. This can be a challenge.

WHAT YOU SHOULD KNOW:
There are a lot of directions you can take if you want to be a landscape architect. You can work only on big national parks, or you can be a city planner, or you can do garden design. Or you can work on all of these.

As far as school goes, you can combine a degree in landscape architecture with your undergraduate work in a four- or five-year program.

Or you can enroll in a graduate program, which is two or three years. It's possible to get into landscape architecture without a degree, but you have to apprentice for so long that it's really not worth it, and the licensing exam would be very difficult to pass without school.

All firms are different when it comes to the work environment. At some firms, you work a sixty-hour week. But I work a forty-hour week, normally 8:00 A.M. to 4:00 P.M. We think that if you burn out on your work you won't be creative.

The pay is comparable to that of an architect. It's not in the league of investment banking. Few of us get fame and fortune, but you can earn a good living in this field. You also get real satisfaction. It's nice at the end of a day to see a tangible thing you've produced. You can walk through a space you've helped create, see that it looks good and works well, and know that the client is happy. You feel you've really done something.

Anne may use aspects of old plans in new designs.

"Every year, and with every crop, things change."

CAROLYN HEDBERG

PLANT GROWER

Litchfield, Connecticut

WHAT I DO:

I'm the head grower for a plant nursery that sells both through the mail and through our retail store. We sell potted plants grown in our greenhouses as well as bare-root plants, which are taken straight from the fields.

As head grower, I'm responsible for the twenty greenhouses and the plants that are grown in them. My work includes all the day-to-day activity you might expect: checking all the plants and making sure that they're watered and fertilized. Beyond that, however, there's a lot of scheduling and coordinating to be done. For example, since we're a year-round operation, I schedule the opening of the greenhouses in the spring and the covering of them in the fall.

Caroline inspects one of the many plants in the greenhouse.

If we don't cover the greenhouses before the temperature drops, the plants that aren't frost-hardy will die.

HOW I GOT STARTED:

In high school, I decided that if I was going to spend so much of my life at my job, I wanted it to be something that I really enjoyed. I already liked gardening, having spent some time rescuing my mother's house plants, but I was also interested in sales. I thought I would work either in the retail end of clothing or in plants.

In college, I got a degree in plant science. After that, I worked at a nursery that did a little bit of everything. They did plant retailing, plant wholesaling, and even landscaping. They had all sorts of plants including potted plants, foliage plants, and cacti. Working there, I got a little taste of everything and a lot of valuable experience.

My next job was here. I started as a grower twelve years ago and then moved up.

HOW I FEEL ABOUT IT:
This is a fun job because it's never the same. Every year, and even with every crop, things change. One part of my job is anticipating those changes and preparing for them.

WHAT YOU SHOULD KNOW:
While getting a degree is important because it helps you understand why plants act a certain way, there's nothing like real-world experience. Try to work in a plant nursery part-time while you're in school and also during the summer. At my nursery, we hire high school students, and we're also trying to work out an internship program with colleges. Other nurseries have similar programs.

Because plants don't stop growing, there's always something to do. So even on weekends, you've got to have someone come in and take care of watering, ventilating, and heating. We try to keep our hours to about forty a week, but at the height of the spring season, some people can work seventy hours a week.

The pay scale for horticulture isn't that high. Here, we start people at $7 an hour. If you do well, and end up managing a plant nursery, you can make $30,000 to $40,000 a year, depending on the size of the nursery.

Caroline makes sure the plants are properly watered.

Related Careers

Here are more outdoor-related careers you may want to explore:

ARCHITECT
Architects design homes and office buildings and work with contractors to oversee their construction.

ASTRONOMER
Astronomers study and observe the size, distance, and movement of such celestial bodies as comets, planets, and stars.

BICYCLE TOUR LEADER
Bicycle tour leaders plan the routes of the trips they lead and oversee them to make sure that none of the cyclists gets lost or injured.

CAMP DIRECTOR
Camp directors coordinate all the activities at a summer camp, including overseeing the campers' housing and meals, managing the staff, and performing the administrative work.

CHRISTMAS TREE GROWER
Christmas tree growers plant and raise pine, fir, and spruce trees that are harvested each fall for use as Christmas trees.

CRUISE DIRECTOR
Cruise directors organize and carry out all the social and recreational activities that take place aboard cruise ships.

FARMER
Farmers cultivate the land and raise not only food crops but also fiber crops such as cotton.

LANDSCAPE CONTRACTOR
Landscape contractors use plans designed by landscape architects to plant trees and flowers in gardens and public spaces.

LIFEGUARD
Lifeguards watch over beaches and pools to ensure the safety of swimmers. They are trained in water rescue and first aid.

SAILING INSTRUCTOR
Sailing instructors teach people how to sail all types of boats, as well as how to maintain water safety.

SPELUNKER
Spelunkers specialize in the study and exploration of caves and other subterranean regions.

SURVEYOR
Surveyors observe and map the landscape, marking the contours of the land as well as roads and property boundaries.

Organizations

Contact these organizations for information about the following careers:

RANGER
American Forestry Association
1319 18th Street, N.W., Washington, D.C., 20036

ZOO CURATOR
American Society of Zoologists
104 Sirius Circle, Thousand Oaks, CA 91360

PLANT GROWER
American Society for Horticultural Science
113 South West Street, Alexandria, VA 22314

FISHING GUIDE
Future Fishermen Foundation
One Berkeley Drive, Spirit Lake, IA 51360

WINEMAKER
Geneva Experimental Station
Department of Horticultural Sciences, Geneva, NY 14456

MARINE ARCHAEOLOGIST
Mel Fisher Maritime Heritage Society
200 Greene Street, Key West, FL 33040

ORGANIC FARMER
National Future Farmers of America Organization
Box 15160, National FFA Center, Alexandria, VA 22309

RANGER
National Park Service/U.S. Department of the Interior
C Street between 18th and 19th Streets, N.W., Washington, DC 20240

RECREATION DIRECTOR
National Recreation and Park Association
1601 North Kent Street, Arlington, VA 22209

SKI PATROL
National Ski Patrol System
133 South Van Gordon Street, Lakewood, CO 80228

LANDSCAPE ARCHITECT
Pennsylvania State University/Department of Landscape Architecture
210 Unit D, University Park, PA 16802

COAST GUARD SEAMAN
U.S. Coast Guard
Washington, DC 20590

Books

AGRICULTURE CAREERS
By Gene and Clare Gurney. New York: Franklin Watts, 1978.

AIM FOR A JOB IN CATTLE RANCHING
By Oren Arnold. New York: Richards Rosen, 1971.

**THE CAREER CHOICES ENCYCLOPEDIA:
GUIDE TO ENTRY-LEVEL JOBS**
By Career Associates. New York: Walker & Co., 1986.

**CAREER GUIDE 2000: FISHERY, FORESTRY, WILDLIFE,
AND RELATED OCCUPATIONS**
By W.J. Hoagman. Hayes, Va.: Remington House, 1977.

THE COMPLETE CAREER GUIDE
By David M. Brownstone and Gene R. Hawes. New York:
Simon & Schuster, 1980.

THE COMPLETE GUIDE TO ENVIRONMENTAL CAREERS
Washington, D.C.: Island Press, 1989.

FORESTRY AND ITS CAREER OPPORTUNITIES
By Ralph D. Nyland, Charles C. Larson, and Hardy L. Shirley.
New York: McGraw-Hill, 1983.

GUIDE TO OUTDOOR CAREERS
By Martha Thomas. Harrisburg, Pa.: Stackpole Books, 1981.

OPPORTUNITIES IN AGRICULTURE CAREERS
By William C. White and Donald N. Collins. Lincolnwood, Ill.:
VGM Career Horizons, 1988.

OPPORTUNITIES IN MARINE AND MARITIME CAREERS
By William Ray Heitzmann. Lincolnwood, Ill.: VGM Career Horizons, 1988.

OPPORTUNITIES IN PART-TIME AND SUMMER JOBS
By Adrian Paradis. Lincolnwood, Ill.: VGM Career Horizons, 1987.

THE OUTDOOR CAREERS GUIDE
By Gene R. Hawes and Douglass L. Brownstone. New York:
Facts on File, 1986.

THE TEENAGE EMPLOYMENT GUIDE
By Allan B. Goldenthal. New York: Monarch Press, 1983.

THE TEENAGER'S GUIDE TO THE BEST SUMMER OPPORTUNITIES
By Jan W. Greenberg. Boston: Harvard Common Press, 1985.

Glossary Index